THE HUMAN MANDOLIN

THE HUMAN MANDOLIN

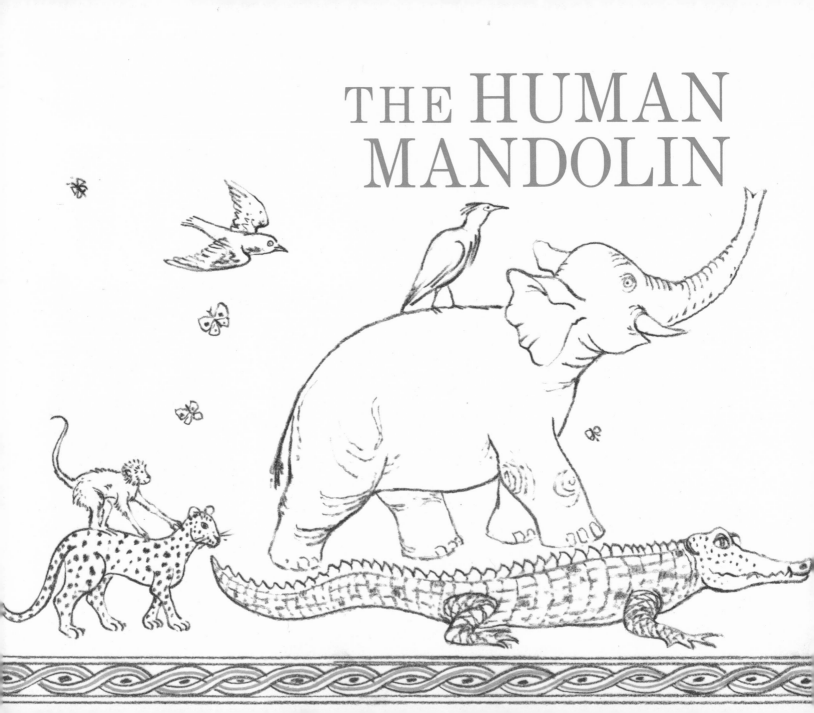

by MOSES L. HOWARD • *illustrated by* BARBARA MORROW

HOLT, RINEHART AND WINSTON
New York   Chicago   San Francisco

Published simultaneously in Canada by Holt, Rinehart and
Winston of Canada, Limited.

Library of Congress Cataloging in Publication Data
Howard, Moses L, date
    The human mandolin.
    SUMMARY: The old musician puts into the mandolin
the most beautiful and joyous sounds he can find.
    [1. Music—Fiction] I. Morrow, Barbara, illus.
II. Title.
PZ7.H834Hu   [E]   74-3122
ISBN 0-03-012961-3

Typography by Barbara Morrow
Printed in the United States of America: 070/074
First Edition

For Jennifer Osborne
and the Seth Low Music Lovers:
    Beah Shuttleworth and
    Ethel Feagley

                M.H.

For Bob with love

                B.M.

Once there lived a great musician who could make and play many musical instruments. He took reeds and trees and from them made flutes, drums, xylophones, and mandolins. He would rub his old, gnarled hands across their smoothness, and the wrinkles in his face would dance in a merry grin.

Early in the morning, when tears of gladness hung on the grass and the animals ran about seeking breakfast, the old musician would greet them. He found songs in their greetings and in the laughter of children, and he made notes of this music and played it on his xylophones.

Through the day he worked under a big tree near a village. When he was not whittling or sanding, or stretching strings or hides on drums, he played music and people came to listen. Sometimes he would lay aside his work and go from village to village. While people worked, he joined in the planting or weeding or harvesting. When they needed rest, he would play to them and sing with them and tell them stories of their greatness. The villagers were happy whenever he came.

As time passed, the villages grew into towns. People traveled in fast cars instead of on bicycles or on foot. They hurried to work in factories, then hurried home to eat and sleep. They passed by the little musician as he worked on his instruments under the ancient tree where man was born.

The old musician longed to beat the drums, strike the xylophone, or strum the strings of his mandolins, but there was no one to listen. Sometimes he played for himself. But that only made him sad.

One day he got an idea! He would make the best mandolin he had ever made. And into it he would put the sweetest sounds in the world. Then the music could be kept in the mandolin until people were ready to listen to it again.

He chopped down the tallest and straightest tree, which had been singing and dancing in the wind all of its life, and began to carve it on his workbench. The sun was his torch, the moon his candle, as he chiseled and carved, chiseled and carved. He shaped the mandolin like his body. He gave it a long, gnarled neck and a small head, and a mouth creased in a smile—both sad and happy. The strings ran from neck to stomach. The old musician chanted while the old hands moved over the wood.

When the mandolin was finished, he set out early to collect the music. Deep in the woods, among the tall trees, he found the welcome bird, the dove, and the bird of paradise. And he asked the birds to sing. He did not take the first notes but waited until the birds' songs set the forest leaves to shaking joyfully.

He took the merriest notes and rubbed them into the
great mandolin.

He thanked the birds and went on to the lake.

"Will you give me your happy splashing sounds that sometimes tinkle like bells?" he asked. The lake asked the musician to wait for the wind, saying that the lake and the wind usually sang a duet.

The old man was glad to do so. He had an enjoyable time with the two friends, then went away with their voices in the mandolin. On his way home, the wind hummed merrily over the grass for him. This sound, too, he put into the mandolin. Then he caught the brightness of the sun and drifting blue clouds, and pressed these in too.

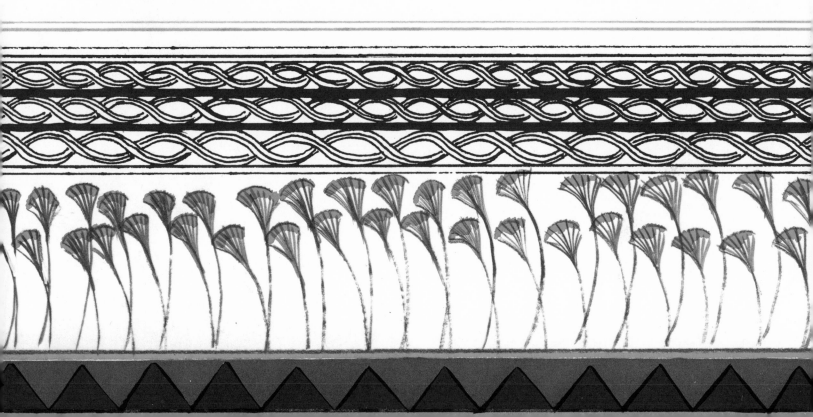

Now happy sounds filled his mandolin. But there was yet one sound missing—the sound of laughter. He went from village to village, through forests and over wide grasslands, passing zebra, lion, leopard, and buffalo. He heard the playful chatter of monkeys and the evening trumpeting of elephants, but no laughter.

Then the old man came near a tall stand of elephant grass and heard flute notes that made his heart jump and his weary legs springy. Before him was a herd of goats. The goat herders played their flutes, laughing and urging each other on.

The old musician quite forgot his age as he joined in, first with his flute, then with his mandolin. When he left the village, his mandolin was expanded with sounds of laughter.

Finally, the mandolin was finished. How beautiful it was! So smooth and brown. When he tapped it with his thumb it gave a rich, bass sound. And when he plucked the strings, the sweet notes set his heart fluttering.

At night, sitting under his tree, he began to play, and a strange and wonderful thing happened. As he strummed the mandolin in the moonlight he got smaller and smaller. Soon he was much smaller than the mandolin. While he still could, he plucked a string. And, as it vibrated, he skipped onto a note, then slid down the string and into the mandolin.

The old musician's drums, xylophones, flutes, hand organs, and mandolin lay under the tree where he had left them. One day, a thief came and took them away in a sack. He had customers who would buy the xylophones, drums, and flutes. But he knew no one who would buy the mandolin. On his way out of town, he flung the mandolin on a junk heap.

There the smooth, brown mandolin rested until a country man, returning from market on his bicycle, saw the shining wood and took it home. That night in his hut the man drank too much beer. He tried to play the mandolin, but the sounds would not come. In his drunkenness he put the mandolin up in the roof beams of his hut and forgot about it. And there it stayed, gathering dust and spiderwebs.

A time came when sickness gripped the towns and the whole country. There were few farmers and not enough food. Hunger was everywhere. People fell sick and died. Finally a wise leader said some people must go back to the land to grow food. No one wanted to go but hunger, with his strong lash, beat people from the town and drove them back to the country.

They found the villages overgrown with bush, grass, and weeds. But soon voices were heard in the villages, and the sounds of axes, hoes, and knives sang over the land. They worked from morning to evening, digging, planting, weeding—hunger pushed them on.

The plants grew. When the harvest came, crops were
good, with much grain and roots, and the people had
food to eat.

In the evenings, in the open places, in front of family huts, the adults rested while children watched their goats or made up games.

One evening while chasing each other they ran into a hut and spied something overhead among the cobwebs. One boy climbed on an old broken bench and brought the wooden object down.

A little girl brushed the cobwebs and dust from the smooth, brown wood, and seeing it was a mandolin, strummed it. A beautiful thing happened. The mandolin began to play by itself, making the most charming sounds. It made sounds of sighing lake water, sounds like birds' songs, sounds of happy chattering monkeys, and sounds like the sun on bright rocks and the wind in the grass. The adults heard the voices of laughing children and came to listen.

The people tell different stories about what happened in that hut. Some say a tiny wizened man danced out on the strings and played happy tunes. Others said that was not so, but everyone heard the laughing music. And everyone saw the dancing shadow of an old musician on the wall.

From that time on, if a laughing child or a merry adult plucks the strings of a mandolin, all the beautiful sounds collected by the old musician come floating out. Sometimes, in a certain light, when the faces of the listeners are happy, the shadow of the old musician can be seen dancing on the wall.

About the Author

Moses L. Howard has studied in both England and the United States. A former teacher in Kampala, Uganda, he has traveled extensively throughout Africa. Mr. Howard, who has also written under the pen name Musa Nagenda, is the author of *The Ostrich Chase* and *Dogs of Fear*. He presently lives and works in Tacoma, Washington.

About the Artist

Barbara Morrow graduated from the Cleveland Institute of Art with a diploma in mural design. In recent years she has left painting, printmaking and part-time teaching of art to return to her first love, books for children. She has illustrated several books, and has written and illustrated *Well Done*, a picture book. Ms. Morrow lives in Kent, Ohio, with her husband and two sons.

About the Book

The illustrations in this book were printed in three colors, pre-separated by the artist. The text and display type were set in Century Expanded, and the book was printed by offset.